Machines to the Rescue

# Rescue Boats

by Bizzy Harris

Bullfrog Books

# Ideas for Parents and Teachers

Bullfrog Books let children practice reading informational text at the earliest reading levels. Repetition, familiar words, and photo labels support early readers.

## Before Reading

- Discuss the cover photo. What does it tell them?

- Look at the picture glossary together. Read and discuss the words.

## Read the Book

- "Walk" through the book and look at the photos. Let the child ask questions. Point out the photo labels.

- Read the book to the child, or have him or her read independently.

## After Reading

- Prompt the child to think more. Ask: Did you know about rescue boats before reading this book? What more would you like to learn about them?

Bullfrog Books are published by Jump!
5357 Penn Avenue South
Minneapolis, MN 55419
www.jumplibrary.com

Library of Congress Cataloging-in-Publication Data

Names: Harris, Bizzy, author.
Title: Rescue boats / by Bizzy Harris.
Description: Minneapolis, Minnesota: Jump!, Inc., [2022]
Series: Machines to the rescue | Includes index.
Audience: Ages 5–8 | Audience: Grades K–1
Identifiers: LCCN 2020041856 (print)
LCCN 2020041857 (ebook)
ISBN 9781645279167 (hardcover)
ISBN 9781645279174 (paperback)
ISBN 9781645279181 (ebook)
Subjects: LCSH: Search and rescue boats—Juvenile literature.
Classification: LCC VM466.S4 H37 2022 (print)
LCC VM466.S4 (ebook) | DDC 363.28/60284—dc23
LC record available at https://lccn.loc.gov/2020041856
LC ebook record available at https://lccn.loc.gov/2020041857

Editor: Jenna Gleisner
Designer: Molly Ballanger

Photo Credits: silvergull/Shutterstock, cover; Joseph Mercier/Dreamstime, 1; Sergiy1975/Shutterstock, 3; Douglas Litchfield/Shutterstock, 4; U.S. Coast Guard, 5, 6–7, 8–9, 16–17, 19, 20–21, 23tr, 23bm, 23br; Iakov Filimonov/Shutterstock, 10, 23tm; KPegg/Shutterstock, 11; U.S. Army National Guard, 12–13; U.S. Army, 14–15, 23tl; E. O./Shutterstock, 18; Shutterstock, 22, 23bl; Andrey Ezhov/Shutterstock, 24.

Printed in the United States of America at Corporate Graphics in North Mankato, Minnesota.

# Table of Contents

On the Water .................................................. 4

Rescue Boat Tools ........................................ 22

Picture Glossary .......................................... 23

Index ............................................................... 24

To Learn More ........................................... 24

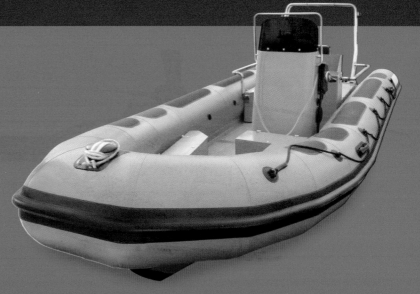

# On the Water

Zoom!
Here comes
a rescue boat!

Why?

Another boat needs help.

wave

These boats go over waves.
Wow!

Operators drive.
They use radar.
It helps them
find their way.

# Motors are in back.

motor ·····▶

# They move the boats fast.

This boat helps
in a flood.

A car can't drive
in the water.

But a boat can!

It rescues people.

13

This crew uses oars.

They paddle.

oar

life vest

FIRST AID KIT

first aid kit

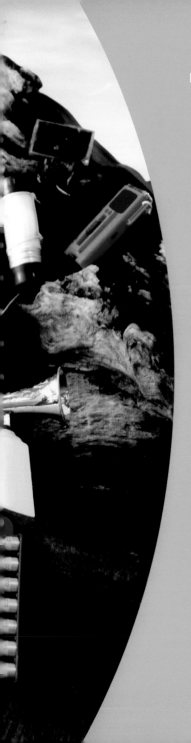

These boats carry supplies.

Like what?

They have life vests.

They have first aid kits.

# They have life buoys, too.

life buoy ·····▷

This crew throws one.
It floats.

The person holds on.

He is safe!

# Rescue Boat Tools

**Take a look at some of the tools found in a rescue boat!**

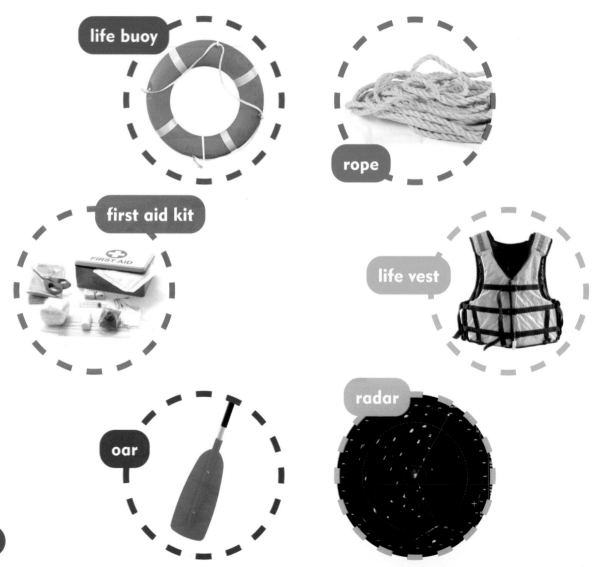

life buoy

rope

first aid kit

FIRST AID

life vest

oar

radar

# Picture Glossary

**crew**
The group of people who operate a boat, plane, or train.

**motors**
Machines that produce motion or power.

**operators**
People who work certain machines, devices, or vehicles.

**radar**
A device used to detect moving things in the distance.

**rescues**
Saves from danger.

**supplies**
Things that are needed for a particular job.

# Index

crew 14, 19

drive 8, 13

first aid kits 17

flood 13

help 5, 8, 13

life buoys 18

life vests 17

motors 10

oars 14

operators 8

radar 8

waves 7

# To Learn More

**Finding more information is as easy as 1, 2, 3.**

❶ Go to www.factsurfer.com

❷ Enter "rescueboats" into the search box.

❸ Choose your book to see a list of websites.